BIRTHDAY at the PANDA PALACE

by Stephanie Calmenson
illustrated by Doug Cushman

HarperCollinsPublishers

For Annabelle Helms
–S.C.

To Erzsi and the
missed birthday party
–D.C.

Manufactured in China.

For information address HarperCollins Children's Books, a division of HarperCollins Publishers, 1350 Avenue of the Americas, New York, NY 10019. www.harpercollinschildrens.com
Library of Congress Cataloging-in-Publication Data
Calmenson, Stephanie.
Birthday at the Panda Palace / by Stephanie Calmenson ; illustrated by Doug Cushman.– 1st ed.
p. cm. Summary: During Mouse's birthday celebration at the Panda Palace restaurant all of her animal friends bring gifts, but the best present of all arrives last.
ISBN-10: 0-06-052663-7 – ISBN-10: 0-06-052664-5 (lib. bdg.)
ISBN-13: 978-0-06-052663-4 – ISBN-13: 978-0-06-052664-1 (lib. bdg.)
[1. Mice–Fiction. 2. Birthdays–Fiction. 3. Gifts–Fiction. 4. Animals–Fiction. 5. Stories in rhyme.]
I. Cushman, Doug, ill. II. Title.
PZ8.3.C13Bir 2007 [E]–dc22 2005017795

1 2 3 4 5 6 7 8 9 10
❖
First Edition

The Panda Palace opened
For a party at noon.
Balloons and streamers
Danced round the room.

It was Mouse's birthday.
Her friends brought her in.
Mr. Panda said, "Welcome!
Let the party begin!"

They started with games.

They played "Do What You See."

Mouse got to be leader.

She said, "Follow me!"

After games came the presents,
Green, red, yellow, blue.
Mr. Panda said, "Mouse,
These are all just for you!"

The first gift was Elephant's.
He said, "When it gets hot,
I use my nose for a hose.
That cools me a lot.

"But Mouse, you can't do that,

So here is the plan:

Whenever you're hot,

You can use your new . . .

"Fan!"

The lions roared proudly,
"As Queen and as King
We wanted to get you
Just the right thing.

"We love you so much,
We shopped all over town.
You'll be a true princess
With this shiny gold . . .

"Crown!"

"We tried building with straw.
We tried building with sticks.
Then we pigs decided
We'd better use bricks.

"It's stronger than strong.
It's just for you, Mouse.
We hope you like having
Your own little . . .

"House!"

"For monkeys like us,
Bananas will please.
But for you, birthday mouse,
Here's a big chunk of . . .

"Cheese!"

"Giraffes, as you know,
Stand up very tall.
While you, our dear mouse,
Even standing, are small.

"This gift has a string.
When you put it in flight,
It goes higher than us.
It's a mouse-size . . .

"Kite!"

"Hyenas like laughing,
So what did we do?
We made something funny.
Now you can laugh too.

"Tear off the wrapping.
Go on, take a look.
There are pages and pages
Of jokes in this . . .

"Book!"

Where was the mouse when the lights went out?

In the dark.

What do you do with a blue mouse?

Cheer her up.

What is a mouse's favorite game?

Hide-and-squeak!

"The Honey Bear All-Stars
Are the best team of all.
We won the World Series.
Here's our autographed . . .

"Ball!"
I'm worried.
My surprise for
Mouse is *very* late.
This party is
a home run!

The chicks started singing,

"Deedle-dee, peep!

This musical present

Is for you to keep.

"You can make music

That's your very own.

Play a tune for us, Mouse,

On your new . . .

"Xylophone!"
Deedle-dee, dee! Happy birthday to me!

Mouse thanked every friend.
She said, “You are all great!”
But Mr. Panda was worried.
His surprise gift was late.

Then the door slowly opened.
They heard a tiny voice wail,
“It's me, Mouse! I made it!”
It was Mouse's friend . . .

Surprise!
"Snail!"
Happy Birthday, Mouse!
Hooray! How did you get here? You live so far away!

"I'm your gift from Mr. Panda.
He sent his pickup truck.
We hit a nasty pothole and
The pickup truck got stuck!
"I walked and I walked
As fast as I could go,
But fast for a snail
Is still very slow."
You can rest later in my new brick house.

Mouse said, "Thank you, Mr. Panda!

I can't believe my eyes.

You brought my friend from far away.

Snail's the best surprise!"

Mr. Panda said, "I've one more gift.

You know I love to bake.

At last we're all together.

Waiters, roll out the birthday . . .

"Cake!"

Mouse's friends sang "Happy Birthday."

They said, "Make a wish and blow!"

They ate their cake with ice cream

And got goody bags to go.

So on *your* next birthday,
If you're going that way,
Just see Mr. Panda.
Here's what he'll say:

“At the Palace we know
How special you are.
That’s why on your birthday,
You are the . . .

"STAR!"